I Was There...

RICHARD III

While this book is based on real characters and actual historical events,
some situations and people are fictional, created by the author.

Scholastic Children's Books
Euston House,
24 Eversholt Street
London, NW1 1DB, UK

A division of Scholastic Ltd
London ~ New York ~ Toronto ~ Sydney ~ Auckland
Mexico City ~ New Delhi ~ Hong Kong

First published in the UK by Scholastic Ltd, 2014

ISBN 978 1407 14504 4

Printed and bound by CPI Group (UK) Ltd, Croydon, CR0 4YY

1 3 5 7 9 10 8 6 4 2

I Was There...

RICHARD III

Stuart Hill

SCHOLASTIC

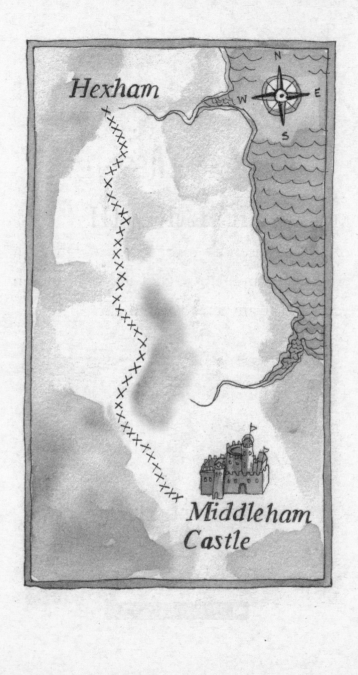

CHAPTER ONE

My name is Richard Plantagenet, Prince of the House of York. I'm the Duke of Gloucester and, although I am only eleven years old, I am already a knight.

I live in Middleham Castle in Yorkshire, where I'm under the protection of the Earl of Warwick, which means I live in his household as his 'ward'. This makes him responsible for my training and education, and this is why, like many other aristocratic boys, I'm also being trained to be a soldier. But so far I haven't drawn my sword in battle.

I don't mean I haven't any experience of the war; that's been part of my life since the day I was born. There have been two powers fighting for the crown ever since my father, the Duke of York, proved he had more right to rule than the King, Henry VI. Those who support Henry call themselves the Lancastrians of the House of Lancaster, and we are the Yorkists of the House of York. The two sides have been fighting on and off for over nine years now and, like all wars, power and victory swings from one side to the other.

This fact was made very clear to me when my father died fighting for the crown in the Battle of Wakefield in 1460. I had to flee for my life with my mother and my brother George to the Low Countries, an area made up by the lands of Belgium, Luxemburg and the Netherlands.

People ask me if I was sad when my father was killed and if I miss him, and of course I do, but he was a man of power and rule and I hardly ever saw him. His life was spent helping to govern the country and then struggling to gain the right to rule. Being a prince makes you different; you live your life in ways that others probably can't understand. You are brought up knowing that you have the right to power, and you're taught that this, along with honour, are the two most important things in life.

But fortunes have a habit of changing swiftly in times of war. After my father died, my older brother, Edward, became the head of the House of York, and soon won a great victory over the Lancastrians at the Battle of Mortimer's Cross in Herefordshire.

Of course it didn't end there, and the Lancastrians beat us at St Albans. The entire country was in chaos, nobody knew who really held power, but then when the city of London gave support to my brother, the Battle of Towton soon followed. Once again, Edward was victorious after a vicious struggle in which thousands died. He was declared King in 1461, and since then most of the fighting has stopped.

All of this meant I was able to come home to England again. So as you can see, I've known all about the war ever since I could think for myself and understand what people around me were saying.

But actually taking part in the fighting itself... that's different. That's completely different.

As I've already said, like all boys of my age and from my background, I'm training as a soldier, a process that began over two years ago when I was nine years old. I can use a sword and dagger, a mace (or war-hammer), ride a warhorse and shoot a longbow (the full-size bow and arrow used in battle) better than almost anyone else my age. But I've yet to use these skills in a real battle. Training with a professional soldier called a Sergeant-at-Arms who knows you and treats you with respect because you're the King's brother is obviously nothing like a real battle where people want to kill you. So I don't know how I'd react; would I freeze and not be able to even lift a sword, as sometimes happens?

Would I be a coward and run away? And if I did neither of these things and fought like a Prince of the House of York really should, how would I feel if I killed a man?

Well, one May morning in 1464 a series of events began that would quickly lead me to my first battle, where I'd find the answers to all of these questions.

I have my own rooms in the main keep of Middleham Castle. This is the huge square building like a tower often found in the heart of a castle. It has massively high and thick walls, slit windows for archers to shoot from and a fighting platform at the very top where soldiers can defend the castle from attackers behind the protection of the strong battlements that run around the very top of the wall and stick up like square teeth. Here the defenders can shoot arrows down on the enemy and then hide from any returned fire. But the keep is also the place where the Earl of Warwick and other members of the household have their quarters. Most of them are luxurious, with fine furnishings, tapestries and in some cases even carpets, instead of the woven mats that are made of the rushes that grow along the riverbank.

My rooms are amongst the best in the entire keep, but on that particular May morning I didn't have time to think of anything but my lessons. I was sitting at a table reading boring law books in preparation for Master Guillard's lesson. I suppose Master Guillard is a good man… in his way. Like most tutors he's a priest, and he's almost as dry and dusty as his books. If you get anything wrong in his lessons, his face shrivels up in disapproval like an apple that's been in the store cupboard for too long. And then he'll have what he calls "a quiet word" with my guardian, the Earl of Warwick.

I was determined this wasn't going to happen today, so I tried to concentrate on the boring tangle of French and Latin words. A sudden thump on my door made me spin round in my chair as Francis Lovell almost leapt into my room.

Baron Francis Lovell is my closest friend and after his father died he also became a ward of the Earl of Warwick, just like me. We were always playing jokes on each other, but he wasn't joking now. His face was red with excitement:

"The Lancastrians are moving! There's going to be a battle!"

I leapt to my feet, knocking over my chair with a clatter. Our enemy was looking for a fight again. "Where?"

"Not sure yet, but somewhere near

Hexham. Our army's marching out to stop them; a messenger's just arrived. He said they should catch up with them there!"

"Where exactly is the messenger? What else did he say?" I could feel that my face was as red as my friend's, and for a moment I almost forgot the pain in my back caused by the curve of my spine that no doctor has been able to do anything about.

"He's in the Great Hall with the Earl of Warwick. They were still talking about soldiers and equipment when I came to get you. I think we're sending a small troop of knights to help. COME ON!"

Francis rushed to the door and then, remembering, stopped and turned to wait for me. I hated it when people treated me differently because of my back, so I waved him on impatiently. The physicians may think that the curve in my spine's getting slowly worse, but I was determined not to let it slow me down.

When we reached the Great Hall it seemed to be full of everyone who lived in Middleham castle, from the Commander of the Guard, to the lowliest of the kitchen drudges, but it was eerily silent as everyone strained to hear what the messenger had to say. I strode forward knowing they'd part to let me through; I am the brother of the King after all.

We reached the centre of the hall where Richard Neville, the Earl of Warwick, sat in a high-backed chair. The messenger stood in front of Warwick like a schoolboy trying to explain to the master why he hadn't learnt his lessons, but he immediately stopped talking when he saw people bowing to me and parting to let me through.

"Ah Richard! I'm glad you're here, this'll be of interest to you," said the Earl in his usual cool tones. "And to your shadow, Lovell." When he smiled, his mouth curled, but his eyes never stopped watching you.

I've heard many people describe Warwick as a pleasant man, but I think he's cold and uses his smile and false friendliness to get the power and wealth he wants.

He stood and bowed his head to me, then waved up a chair.

"My back's not so crippled that I need to sit, my Lord Earl," I said quietly.

"I had thought of no such a thing," Warwick answered. "I've been sitting as you can see, and I'm as healthy as a bull."

"But old, or at least older than me."

The Earl looked at me. "Older is certainly true."

"Francis, there's a chair here for you," I said, turning to my friend and holding his eye.

Lovell nodded and secretly smiled. "Thank you, my Lord Prince, and thank you too, my Lord Earl." He emphasised the titles to show who was more powerful.

Warwick frowned for a moment, knowing we were trying to make him look small, but he was too clever to show his feelings for long, and he bowed his head again, then waved Francis to the chair.

Warwick turned back to the messenger who stood waiting patiently. He was obviously a soldier and wore a surcoat, which is a loose robe, over a shirt of mail under his travel-stained cloak. "Go on with what you were saying," the Earl ordered.

"Almost all's been said, my Lord," the man answered. "The enemy's force is quite small, between five and eight thousand men; we expect to intercept them somewhere near Hexham, unless they change course."

Warwick looked thoughtful, then he turned and looked directly at me. "A force of eight thousand… A good size for a pair of young soldiers in training to earn their blooding."

"You're going to send us to the battle?" I asked, unable to keep the excitement out of my voice. Every young soldier dreams of his 'blooding', the time when he fights his first battle and kills his first man.

"You and an escort of a hundred or so cavalry, yes. You're a little young yet to fight, but you can witness the action from close range and see exactly what happens on the dance floor of war. My brother, John Neville, commands our force; I'll send word that you and Baron Lovell are on your way."

I looked at Francis and grinned and he nodded happily back. We were going to battle! Now we'd find out if all the training had worked. Now we'd find out if we were really soldiers of the House of York!

CHAPTER TWO

We couldn't wait to get out of the Great Hall and back to my chamber so that we could discuss it all. As we hurried away through the crowds, a young girl stepped out in front of us. She'd been hidden away amongst the shadows near the door, but she stepped into the light and smiled.

It was Anne Neville and, even though she was the Earl of Warwick's daughter, she was kind, generous and our friend. I seized her hand and dragged her along with us. "Where's your chaperone?" I asked, knowing that all young ladies always had an older attendant to make sure nothing happened to them.

"She thinks I'm in my chambers practising my embroidery."

"So why aren't you?" Francis asked.

"Boring!"

"It might be boring, but it's what young aristocratic ladies are expected to do," he answered as we hurried along the winding corridors of the castle and out into the courtyard.

"Perhaps so, but it's still boring, so when I heard a messenger had arrived I thought I'd sneak in to hear what he had to say and to find out what you and Richard were doing."

"That's Prince Richard to you, Mistress Anne Neville," said Francis. "And I'm Baron Lovell, in fact I'm the eighth Baron Lovell."

By this time we'd crossed the courtyard and were climbing the spiral staircase in the keep that led to my chamber, but Anne, who was as clever as a family of foxes, managed to curtsy in an exaggerated manner.

"Please forgive me, my Lords," she said sarcastically. "How could I not have noticed how wonderful and superior you both are? Will you ever forgive me?"

I grabbed her hand again. "Come on, you two can finish bickering later."

When we reached my chambers, there was a soldier guarding my door as usual. The Earl of Warwick said this was because of my status as the King's brother, but it always made me feel like a hostage. I suppose I was being silly, the guard never stopped me coming and going, but I also knew that one word from Warwick could turn my guard into my jailer.

We burst into my rooms and dragged chairs up to the fire that burned brightly in the grate. The Earl was proud of the fact that Middleham Castle had so many chambers with their own fireplaces, but today we weren't interested in the wonders of modern building.

"So what did the messenger say?" Anne asked eagerly.

"You mean you don't know?" I was surprised. "But I thought you were at the back of the hall."

"I was, but with so many people crammed into the place and muffling the voices, I couldn't hear details. All I know is that the Lancastrians are somewhere nearby."

"They're in Northumbria, perhaps a two-day march away," said Francis. "They won't attack here, Middleham's too strong. But there's talk of them advancing on Hexham."

"Hexham? But that already has a strong force of soldiers in case the Scots invade!" said Anne, who never spoke like a girl and had always understood war and politics as well as any boy. She was actually only eight years old but spoke, thought and acted like someone much older. "They'd need a massive army to take the place. Do we know their numbers?"

"Between five and eight thousand," I said.

She snorted just like Warwick, her father. "Then they won't be taking Hexham."

"No," I agreed, "But they are in our territory and their numbers are great enough to be dangerous. That's why an army's being sent to intercept them."

"And me and Richard are going to be part of it!" Francis suddenly blurted.

Anne's hands flew to her mouth and her face went crimson. She obviously hadn't heard that bit of news either. "You and Richard are going to be…!" She turned to me. "Is this true?"

I nodded. "Yes. Your father's sending us with a small force of cavalry to offer support."

She stood and paced between her chair and the window, then she stopped and laughed. "Your first blooding! Oh, I wish I was going with you! You must remember everything and tell me all about it! Write it down if you have to! I want to know every detail; what it feels like, what it sounds like, what it smells like even! Oh I wish, I wish, I wish I was going with you!"

Well you can't," said Francis leaning back in his chair and stretching his feet out to the fireplace. "You're a girl, and girls don't fight."

Anne frowned at him fiercely and I

suddenly felt sorry for her. Daughters of powerful lords like Warwick had no real choice in their lives. When they were young they were taught how to read and after that they learnt to embroider, spin and weave, and perhaps to sing and play prettily on a musical instrument. Then, when they were old enough, they'd be married to some old man to make an alliance between her own family and some other powerful group of lords.

"If girls did fight I'm sure you'd be one of the fiercest," I said, wanting to give her something. "And anyway, Francis and I won't be fighting either. We're being sent to watch, that's all."

Francis laughed, "Which is still more than a girl's allowed to do." but Anne ignored him and took my hand for a moment and squeezed it before letting it drop.

"So when do you set out?" she asked, her eyes shining.

"Tomorrow morning at first light." I said.

"I'll be there to see you go," she said determinedly.

"Good, I'd like that." I answered.

CHAPTER THREE

There was still an afternoon of training to be got through before we left, and Sergeant-at-Arms Langham was determined to make sure that Francis and I were truly ready for our first battle. Which meant hard work... and lots of it!

The Earl of Warwick has several boys training to be knights in his household, so when Francis and I walked out into the lists – the fenced-off training ground – the place was crowded with boys practising fighting with the two-handed sword, the mace and the dagger. Off to the side of the yard, the long narrow shooting range called the butts was in use as the servants of knights known as squires and some younger boys called pages practised their skills as archers. Occasionally one of the men-at-arms who were assistants to Sergeant Langham would bawl out someone who'd sent an arrow on a wild flight over the wall and then a boy would go scampering off to make sure he hadn't hit anyone.

Archery is my favourite, and I'm one of the best in the entire castle. Sometimes I can even beat Sergeant Langham in a shoot-off.

But today we were scheduled to practise our equestrian, or horse riding, skills. That meant the dreaded quintain yard!

As we crossed the training ground and headed through the wide gateway into the horse paddock, we stopped to watch as an older boy got ready to tilt at the quintain. He looked incredibly uncertain and awkward as he sized up the high-standing wooden machine with its central post driven deep into the ground, and its wide swivelling arm.

On one end of the arm was the shield the boy would aim for, and on the other the heavy sack full of sand that would swing round dangerously on the end of its rope. The object of the lesson was to charge your horse at the shield and strike it full square with your lance. This made the wooden arm spin wildly and, if you weren't quick enough, the heavy sack on the other end of the arm would swing around and knock you from the saddle!

Francis grabbed my arm. "This should be good," he said with a wicked grin and he nodded at the boy making ready.

I soon saw that he was one of the older boys, in fact a full squire so he must have been sixteen or seventeen years old. I hadn't seen him before, so guessed he had been transferred from one of the Earl of Warwick's other strongholds.

I glanced at Sergeant Langham who stood off to one side bawling orders.

"Come on my Lord of Gisborough; if you take much longer your horse'll be too old to gallop!"

He was the only man I knew who could make a boy's rank and title sound like an insult. I guessed that this was one of many attempts Gisborough had made at the quintain. Usually boys of his age were very well-practised at this sort of thing, but it was plain to see he wasn't a natural horseman, and his horse snorted and sidled as he tried to line his lance up on the target. Obviously Sergeant Langham had singled him out for special treatment. Perhaps he thought he needed the practice.

Gisborough was trying to steady his lance and control what I suspected was one of the more lively horses in the castle stables.

Sometimes Langham liked to have his little joke. I suppose it was his way of keeping aristocratic boys in their place; after all, as a Sergeant-at-Arms it was his duty to train boys who would one day grow up to be the most powerful men in the country. He had to let them know who was boss, at least for the time they were under his command as a teacher in the arts of war.

"He'll never do it," Francis said as we watched the boy trying to balance on the horse's back. "He's bouncing around like a grasshopper on a drum."

"Yes," I agreed. "Let's just hope he's learnt how to fall safely."

"Perhaps you'd like to charge before supper time, my Lord," Langham shouted sarcastically. "Or should we ask one of the younger boys to do it for you?"

That was too much for Gisborough and,

after struggling to level his lance, he spurred the horse. The animal leapt forward and the boy almost fell off backwards, but he steadied himself and, as the quintain loomed over him, he lunged with his lance and hit the shield squarely. But he forgot to crouch low in his saddle and, as the arm of the machine swung around, the heavy sack hit him with a solid thud and knocked him from the saddle.

He landed heavily and lay still, but as we hurried over he sat up, shook himself and coughed.

Sergeant Langham joined us. "Your horse's running loose, my Lord. A good knight thinks of his animal first every time. I suggest you get up and check to see if he's hurt."

I could see the boy was badly winded and, despite being four or five years older than Francis and me, he was desperately trying not to cry. We all need toughening up if we want to be soldiers, but we also need encouragement.

"He did well enough, don't you think, Langham?" I said as I bent and helped the boy to his feet. "It's easy to forget to duck when the arm swings round, and anyway, you seem to have chosen one of the most difficult horses in the stables for him."

The old soldier frowned, but said nothing. "Francis, collect his horse for him," I went on. Then turning to the boy I said: "And I'm sure the Sergeant here will allow you the rest of the day off as you did so well. He's a kind man really and intelligent enough to know when to let a soldier rest and recover."

"Oh, there's no need…" the boy began to protest. "I can carry on."

"I'm sure you can," I said. "But as you must know by now, a true knight is aware of the value of knowing when to withdraw from the battle."

"My Lord Prince I don't think…" Langham began, but before he could finish he was interrupted by the boy dropping to one knee and bowing his head almost into the dirt.

"Prince Richard, forgive me, I had no idea who you were… I mean I've never seen you before… I mean…"

"That's fine, Gisborough, just run along now. I've a feeling Sergeant Langham wants a word with me."

He certainly did. As the older boy disappeared through the archway he rounded on me. Only my position as the King's brother saved me from anything but a good tongue lashing. But I knew that I'd be made to pay for letting the boy off so lightly. And I was also left in no doubt that Langham had little respect for Gisborough or his family. Apparently he wasn't a true aristocrat; his grandfather had been a successful merchant who'd made himself useful to the Royal Court and so had been made a Baronet, which is almost the least important title a man can be given, apart from that of an ordinary knight.

I've often found that men like Sergeant Langham, who come from poor backgrounds themselves, can be the most terrible snobs. Personally I'd sooner a man proved his worth by earning his position in life rather than inheriting it. But as a Prince of the House of York who was born into his status, I don't suppose I'd better say that too loudly.

As I predicted, both Francis and I began to pay for my actions that very afternoon as we tilted at the quintain, practised cavalry moves and fought with the two-handed sword until it was too dark to see.

At one point when the sun had dropped below the castle walls, Francis made a chop at my head with his sword, and I only just parried it in time. The blades were blunted, but a skull could be cracked wide open by a two-handed sword, blunted or not. It was then that Langham was forced to acknowledge it was too dark to carry on and we were at last released from the training grounds.

It was fortunate that we probably wouldn't

see action against the Lancastrians for a couple of days. At least our bruises would have time to heal and some of our stiff muscles would loosen up on the ride.

Still, it was all good practice for our first blooding.

CHAPTER FOUR

I was stiff and sore that night, but I was determined not to miss the evening meal in the Great Hall. It wouldn't be a banquet, as such, but it would be made extra special by the fact a squadron of cavalry would be heading off to do battle the following day.

I wanted to put on a good show and so dressed in my best clothes and even decided to put on the thin circlet of gold that is worn on the head like a crown by all Princes of the Royal House of York.

When I heard a familiar knock at my door I knew it'd be Francis and I almost laughed out loud when he swept into the room.

Obviously he'd had the same idea as me and was wearing his best clothes along with almost every piece of jewellery he owned. Every finger dripped with gold, he wore no fewer than three brooches of rubies and emeralds and around his neck he wore the heavy gilded chain of the Lovell Barons. Unlike me, he's tall and broad and looked like a decorated tree in all his finery.

"Very impressive," I said with a grin. "Do you think anyone will realize there's a boy under all that metalwork and gemstones?"

He grinned in return: "I just want people to know who I really am. I've been training here as a soldier in Middleham Castle for three years now and that's as long as you. But while everyone knows you're Prince Richard, brother of the King, I could just be a stable boy."

He nodded at me where I stood warming myself next to the fire. "I mean look at you, you're every inch a prince. You're… you're skinny, and you even… move in the way that royalty is supposed to! But put me in the right clothes and I could be the boy who mucks out the pigs!"

"Don't be ridiculous," I said. "You look powerful and lordly; you're already almost as tall as the Earl of Warwick himself, something I'll never be. Do you know how frightening you look when you're in a bad mood? Some of the kitchen drudges take one look and just scurry away."

"That's probably because of my red hair," he answered, grinning again. "Maybe they think my head's on fire."

I laughed, but then said: "Come on, let's go down to supper. I think there's going to be music and jugglers tonight."

When we got down to the Great Hall the place was hazy with smoke that rose to the rafters from the huge fire burning in the hearth in the very centre of the flagstone floor, and every bench and table was occupied. The bottler stood in the very midst of the Great Hall directing everything. He was one of the most important servants in the entire place, and he ran everything in the castle that wasn't to do with fighting and warfare. Even so he reminded me of a general as he ordered his serving chamberlains about like soldiers in his personal army.

Of course the knights of the household were there too and, as the Earl of Warwick was a man of such importance, there were more than a hundred of them occupying the upper tables closest to the raised platform or dais where the Earl himself sat like a king with his court.

A soldier escorted Francis and me into the hall and thumped the butt of his spear on the flagstones when we reached the top dais.

The Earl was dressed splendidly in rich green velvet with a huge yellow hat that seemed almost to reach the rafters. I was told later that it was specially shipped from the best hat-makers in London, and cost more than some people earn in a year. Beside him sat his wife, the lady of the castle and Countess of Warwick, Lady Anne de Beauchamp.

At thirty-eight she was still beautiful, and as fearsome as her husband. She ran the domestic side of the castle with the same sort of discipline usually seen in an army on the march, but it was her daughter who caught my eye. Our own little Anne, who only that morning had been bickering with Francis, had been transformed into a grave and powerful lady of the castle. She wore a dark blue silken gown and a snowy white headdress and she looked on all before her with a stony gaze. I could see now that one day she would be as beautiful as her mother, and when she was grown up she'd break many hearts.

I nodded my head to her as the rules of good manners demanded and she curtsied in return, but then as she rose to her full height again, she winked at me. I nudged Francis but he was completely unaware of me as he stared open-mouthed at the transformed Anne.

"Ah, Prince Richard and the Baron Lovell, please do us the honour of joining us at our table," said the Earl, his face alight with smiles and his eyes darting between Francis and me as though trying to read what we were thinking in our faces.

A chamberlain led us to our seats. My chair stood between Warwick's and his daughter Anne's, and I couldn't help noticing that mine and the Earl's were precisely equal, down to the last ounce of gilding and up to the last fraction in height.

Down in the centre of the hall the bottler now raised his hand and immediately the food was brought in. It was all raised high on the shoulders of the serving men in metal serving dishes and it brought with it the rich scents of roasting meats. Up on the musicians' gallery above the main doors the musicians began to play, and soon the sweet sounds of music mingled with the smoke from the central fire and rose up into the rafters, where the huge oak beams of the roof reached across the wide space from wall to wall in a great leap.

The buzz of voices that had been kept

politely low until now rose up into a sea of sound, and the serving boys were soon scurrying around like busy ants with their tall pitchers of ale and wine. When the servants stepped forward to fill our goblets at the top table, the Earl leaned in close. "If you'll take my advice, my Lord, you'll drink only small beer tonight. It's wise to keep a clear head for your first battle and campaign."

Small beer was drunk by everyone in the castle. It was weak and was thought suitable for even the youngest page and, though I knew Warwick was right, it took all my willpower not to defy him and order strong ale or wine. But in the end common sense won out and I beckoned up the boy with the pitcher of small beer.

I made sure that Francis did the same, and I took some comfort when I noticed that even the knights on the high tables were being careful with their drinking. Obviously experienced warriors knew better than to risk a headache and slow reactions at the beginning of a campaign.

In the end the meal fell short of a full banquet. The food was richer than usual, and there were more dishes to choose from, but the entertainment was limited to the musicians playing in the gallery and the

Earl of Warwick's jester – a man who was about as funny as one of Master Guillard's arithmetic lessons on a wet Wednesday afternoon. Also many of the knights who'd be part of the cavalry I'd be riding with the next day were happy to retire early so that they could get as much sleep as they could before the early morning start.

CHAPTER FIVE

The next day dawned cold and bright, filling the inner keep of the castle courtyard with brilliant sunshine. Our cavalry force was drawn up and ready, filling the sharp clean air with the scents of horses and leather. The long line of knights glittered in the early morning sunlight with every man and horse in full armour. We had to be fully prepared; we were riding out to tackle the enemy and didn't know precisely when we'd meet them.

Francis and I sat at the head of the column next to Sir Roger De Castile, an experienced soldier who commanded the hundred knights of our force. He was a man in his fifties who'd fought in the long wars in France as well as at home and counted members of the French aristocracy amongst those he'd both killed in battle and also called his friends.

"A fine riding day, my Lord," said De Castile. "It's cool enough to keep up a good pace, so we should be in Hexham early tomorrow."

I nodded. "I hope the Lancastrians will wait for us."

"Oh they'll wait for us; any commander who takes the trouble to gather a fighting force will want to use them."

"Will they be a problem for us?" Francis asked. Then obviously thinking this sounded too timid he added, "I mean, will they put up a good fight?"

De Castile nodded. "Well, their force is quite small, but there again, so too is ours, so an even match could make for a hard struggle. And they're commanded by the Earl of Somerset, a man who fights before he thinks. But battles are won with brains as well as the sword, so the day should be ours in the end."

Francis caught my eye; these were hardly the fiery words of a warrior that we'd expected. De Castile might have been talking about getting ready to go shopping in the local market and worrying about the costs. But then the old soldier winked at us.

"Well, as boys who'll one day be men commanding men, I've told you the truth, but now I'll show you how to put fire in soldiers' bellies!"

He swung his warhorse around in a clatter of rattling hooves and armour, stood in his stirrups and drew his sword in a wide sweeping gesture: "Men of the House of York," his deep voice boomed. "We ride now to battle in the name of our rightful sovereign and monarch Edward – by the Grace of God, King and ruler of this land! We ride also in support of England and under the assured protection of Saint George, the patron of the blessed soil on which we stand. A rebel army marches even now upon the loyal town of Hexham and it is our swords alone that will save them from the terror and murderous intent of the enemy! Ride now in support of the people of Hexham! Ride now in support of this righteous cause! Ride now in support of King Edward, England and Saint George!"

His voice rang from the stones of the castle walls and a great cheer rose up from the cavalry, and from the servants and residents of the fortress who stood in a knot on the far side of the courtyard. I ran my eyes over the small crowd hoping to see Anne, but there was no sign of her.

The knights were still cheering, and several of them had drawn their swords and circled them above their heads. De Castile bowed in the saddle in reply and then drew his horse into the head of the column again. He smiled at Francis and me.

"That should keep them going for a while.

Just remember, lads, fighting men like to believe their cause is just and that innocent lives are threatened by the enemy they're about to fight. One good rousing speech is worth a hundred foot-soldiers and at least thirty of our bravest knights riding the very best horses."

I'm not sure how I felt about that; it seemed somehow dishonest. But when I looked at the cheering soldiers it felt wrong to disapprove of their sense of justice, even if it had just been created for them by their commander using fine words.

But before I could think about it anymore, a trumpet sounded from the walls and the Earl and Countess of Warwick emerged from the keep along with Anne. They were all dressed in finery again, just as richly as the night before. They all wore jewels that sparkled and glittered in the early morning light like flames.

Warwick nodded his head graciously and Anne and the countess curtsied deeply. In reply the entire unit of cavalry bowed in their saddles, and all was graceful and well-mannered. It was hard to remember that we were preparing to ride out to war; to fight and kill and in some cases to be killed. I may not have actually fought before, but I'd seen what a battlefield looked like after the fighting had finished, and it wasn't graceful or well-mannered. Dead and dying people weren't bothered by such things.

The Earl led his ladies across the courtyard and soon they stood before De Castile, Francis and me. "Your first battle, my Lord," he said to me. "How do you feel?"

I wasn't sure how to reply. I think it was expected that I should say I was excited and ready to kill the enemy, and that I was desperate to get to the fighting. But for some reason the words wouldn't come. So instead I answered: "I'm enjoying the time of calm before we fight."

The Earl's shifting eyes stopped for once and focused on my face. "Calm in a time of war…?"

De Castile suddenly let out a loud, barking laugh into the silence that had fallen. "Spoken like a true campaigner, my Lord Prince! That's exactly how I feel. We fighting men must find our times of peace wherever we can; they're precious and few in number."

The old warrior laughed again. "Your training has found a veteran in this Royal youth, Warwick, you must be very proud!"

The Earl smiled and his eyes started to rove again. "Indeed yes! As long as the calm doesn't interrupt the fighting."

I leaned from my saddle and stared into

Warwick's face. "I am a fighting Prince of the House of York, and you may rest assured, my Lord, that I will kill everyone and anyone that gets in my way, now and throughout my life."

I saw De Castile nodding quietly out of the corner of my eye, but then he blustered into the silence again. "Come now, the ladies are here and ready to say farewell, let us receive any favours they may want to give."

I sat up straight in my saddle and immediately saw Anne watching quietly. I nodded to her, not knowing what she was thinking, but she smiled in return and stepped forward. She was holding two brightly coloured scarves and, standing between Francis's horse and mine, she handed one to him and the other to me.

"There, you can both carry my favour as you're both my friends," she said.

Francis went red with pleasure, and my own face felt warm too. Only true warriors could expect favours from beautiful ladies of the court. Anne was still a girl of course, but as she was only a year or two younger than us it seemed right and fitting.

We both dismounted so that she could tie the scarves around our arms in the approved manner. Francis was wearing a suit of armour his father had worn when he was a boy, and though it had needed a little adjusting, the armourers in Middleham Castle were highly skilled and there were no obvious joins or metal patches. My own armour, on the other hand, had only just been delivered from armourers in the German lowlands. They'd been sent patterns that gave my exact measurements and, most importantly, showed the curvature that my spine was gradually sinking into. Now when I wore the expertly made breast and back plates, no one could tell that I had any sort of problem with my back. I was just a young knight of the House of York, fit and ready to fight.

Anne finished tying the scarves and stood back to admire them. "There, you carry my favour and honour into battle… bring them back safely."

Francis nodded and then coughed, but I stooped and taking Anne's hand, I kissed it.

I'd no idea I was going to do this, it just happened and all three of us blushed.

Just behind us sat Piers Gisborough, the squire I'd rescued from the quintain yard and Sergeant Langham. I'd been knighted when I was ten years old, so had the right to have a battlefield attendant. Gisborough didn't seem to mind acting as a servant to a knight younger than him; in fact he seemed to swell with pride when I first suggested the idea, and Francis quietly pointed out that acting as squire to a Prince would add to Gisborough's standing amongst the other boys. He would act as my servant when we camped for the night. Anyway, it kept him away from Sergeant Langham for a while, and one day's military action was worth weeks of training.

In an attempt to distract us from my act of kissing Anne's hand, I pointed at the young squire. "Gisborough's going to battle too. Perhaps you have a favour for him as well?"

Anne smiled. She was a kind girl and, not wanting to leave Gisborough out, she took a prettily embroidered handkerchief from her sleeve and handed it to the boy. "Now you bear my honour and favour too. I expect to see them returned safely."

Gisborough immediately tucked the handkerchief into his armour and bowed in his saddle with much more dignity than Francis and I had managed.

A sudden fanfare of trumpets announced that we were finally ready to ride, and we climbed back into our saddles. Anne withdrew to stand with her parents, and the castle servants cheered. With a shout from De Castile, our commander, the column clattered forward in a great jingling and jangling of armour and weapons. I turned in my saddle to wave to Anne, and throwing aside her dignity as the Earl's daughter, she waved madly back. Francis waved too. I think he probably felt just the same as I did: we were leaving behind something we could never get back completely. We were leaving behind our childhoods.

Within moments we'd entered the shadows of the gatehouse and the rattle of iron-shod hooves echoed back at us from the stone walls and roof. Then we were out into the day in a burst of sunshine and the hollow drumming of the drawbridge as we trotted over its wooden slats.

Francis and I were off at last to our blooding, or at least to witness our first real battle.

CHAPTER SIX

We kept up a brisk pace as De Castile had
said we would. The weather had been bright
for the last few days and the roads were dry,
so there was no mud to slow us down. We
made a stirring sight as we trotted by with
our brightly coloured banners and glittering
armour, but the faces of the peasants working
in the fields showed nothing but fear.
Armoured soldiers on the road could only
mean war and all the horror that brought
with it. No one cheered; in a civil war I'd
learned that the ordinary people of the land
tried not to choose sides, in case the one
they gave their support to lost.

De Castile talked almost all the time. He talked about the weather and how it might affect the battle; he talked about the crops in the fields and the prospects for a good harvest; he even talked about music and dancing and the latest fashions coming up from London. Suddenly I realized that our veteran commander, who'd fought in more campaigns than I could even guess at, was nervous, and talking constantly was his way of keeping his nerves under control!

When at last De Castile decided to canter back along the line to check that all was well, I nudged Francis. "I thought he'd never go!"

Francis nodded. "If words were arrows all the Lancastrians would be slaughtered by now."

"You know why of course?"

"Nerves," my friend answered, taking me by surprise.

Somehow I never expected big, powerful Francis to have much time for thinking or to care that much about what was happening around him. Never judge anyone by how they look.

"My father said you should never trust a man who isn't nervous before a fight, because he's either stupid or knows something he's not telling you," Francis went on.

"Knows something he's not telling you? Like what?" I asked.

"Like the fact that he could be planning to join the other side if it looks like they're winning."

I nodded and looked back along the line of our cavalry and realized almost every man was showing signs of nerves: constantly checking equipment, fidgeting in the saddle and continually looking around as though expecting an attack at any moment. And many of our knights were almost as experienced as Castile himself!

"I suppose it's all right for us to feel nervous then?" I said.

"I hope so," Francis answered. "Because I'm as jumpy as a cat in a room full of greyhounds!"

"Well, I'm as worried as a hen in a hungry man's kitchen," I answered, not wanting to be outdone.

"I'm as scared as a pigeon in a pie."

"You'd need a lot of pastry," I said, rapping my knuckles on the huge curve of his breastplate.

"And what would you know about pastry and kitchens, my Lord Prince Plantagenet?" Francis asked with a grin. "I bet you've never been anywhere near a frying pan! You wouldn't know a cooking pot if it dropped on your head!"

"And you would, I suppose, my Lord Baron Lovell."

We carried on like this for the next mile or so, pushing away our own nerves by bickering and giggling and being the boys everyone was always telling us we still were, despite everything that was expected of us.

Gisborough joined in now and then, but he was still a little shy of me, and would only speak when spoken to. Even then he used the sort of language you only ever heard in the most formal occasions. This certainly wasn't a problem for Francis. He'd seen me in almost every state you can think of, and so knew I was just an ordinary boy who just happened to have been born into royalty. And now that my back was slowly getting worse everyone could see I was nothing special.

In fact as the miles rolled slowly by, my back began to ache more and more. Despite my curved spine, I like to think I'm quite fit after all the training, but spending hours in the saddle finds all sorts of muscles in places you never knew existed!

Around midday we at last came to a wide stream that was shallow enough to wade across. De Castile decided we'd water and rest the horses for an hour or so at this point. And almost as an afterthought he also said we could eat and rest too!

I must admit it was quite pleasant having Gisborough running around getting everything. Francis didn't mind either, because the squire had decided to include looking after him in his duties as well!

"Bit grim round here," said Francis, nodding at the surrounding treeless moorland. "The entire place looks completely deserted."

I nodded. Despite the sunshine, a cold wind whipped over the hills and brought with it nothing but the scent of mile after mile of heather. "I'm told it's hard to make a living in these hills; nothing grows easily, and only the toughest sheep can eat its grasses."

I struggled to my feet and waved Gisborough away when he ran up to help. "And on top of all of that, the Scots are always raiding. It takes a special sort to make a life up here."

"You like it though, don't you?" Francis said, surprising me with his brain again.

I laughed. "I do; the people are tough and tell you what they think whether you want to hear it or not. And the land has a wildness that's like nowhere else in England. It would be one of the best things to rule such a place."

"And will you?"

"Rule? I'm just a boy, a child. No child should rule this country even if he has an adult to help him as regent and a council to advise him."

"But you might have to if… if the worse sort of thing happened." Francis insisted.

"You mean if my brother is killed and dies without children to follow him." I said. "Well, if that happens before I'm much older it would be a disaster, for me and for the country; this land needs a strong leader, not a boy." I paused and lowered myself painfully back onto the rock Gisborough had covered with a cloak.

"Anyway, it won't happen." I went on. "This battle we're heading for could be the last of the war, and my brother's as strong as an ox. There's no reason why he shouldn't live for years and have fine strong sons who'll be grown up and ready to rule when he finally leaves us."

That seemed to end the talk for a while and we ate the food Gisborough served us in silence. All around us the knights and squires rested as well as they could, perched on the rocks and boulders that burst out of the tough grass, or eased tired riding muscles by slowly strolling up and down. The horses quietly grazed, managing to look like gentle old farm beasts despite the armour and bright heraldic colours.

For a moment I almost forgot the coming battle but then De Castile suddenly burst into the world, shouting orders and rousing us up. "Mount up, gentlemen and my Lord Prince! The enemy awaits and there are miles to ride!"

Soon we were clattering along the hard rock of the roadway over the moorland. De Castile set a good pace; enough to eat up the miles, but not so fast the horses would be too tired to charge and fight when we found the enemy.

CHAPTER SEVEN

For the rest of that day we headed for Hexham over the high moors. But then, just as the sun was beginning to set, we stopped and the order was given to set up camp.

De Castile had selected a wide flat area directly next to the road, and soon the squires, pages and the few camp-followers who'd been allowed to come with us were scurrying around putting up tents, lighting fires and securely tying and grooming the horses.

De Castile set up strong lines of defence, with large numbers of heavily armed guards at every quarter. And a rota was made that would see the camp protected throughout the night. The Lancastrians wouldn't find it easy to take us by surprise if they were in the area.

Within an hour my large tent and that of Francis, De Castile and several other of the senior knights had been put up. The camp looked like the field at a tournament where knights set up highly decorated tents called pavilions, and where they also hang their shields painted with designs that show who they and their families are. But this wasn't any sort of game.

The atmosphere was quiet and, as the sun sank, an icy wind whipped over the moors, driving most into the shelter of their tents or around the fires. I think many people believe that an army on the march does nothing but drink and sing and have the sort of good time usually found only at feasts and banquets. But this certainly isn't the case, not before a battle anyway. Afterwards, if they've won, I've heard there might be some who try to wash away the horrors of what they've seen with too much drink.

But in my tent, the night before the battle was long. My bed was narrow, though I couldn't really complain; most would be sleeping on the hard ground wrapped in blankets. But as a Prince of the realm my tent and travelling bed had been carried on one of the few wagons we'd brought with us.

Thankfully Gisborough had a straw

mattress that he slept on near the entrance, so I wasn't alone. I think he was still nervous of me, but he was even more nervous of what was coming, so for once he was willing to talk.

"This will be your first battle, I suppose?" I said into the darkness, knowing he wasn't asleep.

"Yes, my Lord," he said. Then after a pause he added: "But I've seen many without actually fighting in them myself. When I was six there was a raid on my home. I saw men killed and injured."

"The enemy was driven off?"

"Yes, they were only a small party who thought they could raid an undefended Yorkist house. They didn't realize my father could fight like a cornered bear and all our servants carried arms. Not many rode away."

"Let's hope the same can be said tomorrow after the battle." I said.

"You're sure it will be tomorrow then?"

"Almost certain. De Castile has sent out scouts to spy out the land and to find the main part of our army. They can't be far away."

"The Lancastrians can't be either." Gisborough replied nervously. "What will we do if we meet them first?"

I shrugged, then realizing he couldn't see me in the dark I added: "I'm not sure; fight if we have to, but it'd be safer to retreat if we can. We'd be heavily outnumbered and if we tried to take on the whole Lancastrian army on our own… well, we wouldn't last very long."

"No, I suppose not." Gisborough replied in a small voice.

"You don't have to worry too much. You'll be acting as my arms bearer on the battlefield; so you won't be in the actual fighting. The only time you might have to go anywhere near is if someone's horse is killed and you're called on to take in a replacement." I paused, realizing this didn't sound very comforting. "But anyway, you're my squire and as I'm not allowed to get too close to the action, neither will you."

"I'm not afraid, my Lord," Gisborough suddenly said determinedly.

"Aren't you? Why not? We're not going on some sort of pleasure ride, you know. People will die on both sides – probably thousands of them. Anyone who's not afraid of that must be mad!"

Gisborough was silent for a while, then said. "Perhaps what I meant to say was I'm afraid, but I'll do whatever I have to do… I'll do whatever I need to do."

I thought about his words carefully "That's different," I said after a while. "Perhaps that's all that can be expected of any of us."

The next day we woke up to news that De Castile's scouts had returned during the night and reported that they'd found our army and that a meeting place had been agreed.

Gisborough looked relieved when he heard, and I suppose I must have too. What I'd said earlier was obviously true. A party of a hundred knights and a few fighting squires would have been crushed by the Lancastrian army if they'd found us first.

CHAPTER EIGHT

The Yorkist army cheered as our knights and squires joined them. To my eyes their numbers seemed endless, strung out as they were along the road that led directly to the town of Hexham, but De Castile insisted it was one of the smallest armies he'd ever ridden with.

Armour glittered in the bright sunlight and flags snapped and rattled in the cold breeze. We might have been small, but I thought just the sight of us would be enough to scare off any enemy.

Before the army set off again, De Castile took me to meet the Commander of our Yorkist force. Of course he should've been brought to meet me as I was a Prince of the Realm, but when on campaign there's no time for many of the usual rules.

As I rode by the long line of soldiers with Francis and De Castile on either side of me, many of the men cheered when they recognized the Royal device on my shield and surcoat. I'd also started to wear my own personal badge of the white boar, and I couldn't help feeling proud as the soldiers stood and shouted in support.

We reached the head of the column

where our commander John Neville sat in conference with his officers. He looked just like a younger version of his brother, the Earl of Warwick. He had the same easy way of telling people what to do, and the same shifting eyes that constantly moved from face to face as though looking for signs of treachery.

I nodded in formal greeting when my name was announced and, though he should have bowed, he barely moved his head. He was mounted and his horse was restless, snorting and sidling as we rode up, so that could've been an excuse for his lack of respect, but somehow I think politeness didn't come easily to the Earl of Warwick's brother.

"My Lord Prince," he said in a surprisingly quiet voice. "The knights you've brought with you are welcome."

I heard Francis take a sharp breath at the insult. Neville seemed to be saying the knights were welcome, but that I wasn't. I reached across and laid my hand on my friend's sword arm.

"I'm pleased to be of service, my Lord Neville. De Castile had already told me that you only had a small command, and I see he wasn't wrong. I hope our insignificant addition of knights and squires won't be too much trouble for you."

The shifting eyes stopped and focused on me. Obviously he was a proud man and understood an insult when it was given. For a moment I thought he was actually going to draw his sword, and I tightened my hold on Francis's arm.

But then he seemed to force himself to relax, and he suddenly smiled. "How is your back, my Lord? I hope it doesn't affect your abilities too much."

"My abilities are the equal of men twice my age, my Lord Neville," I answered quietly. "My back is not a problem."

"Then you are a warrior indeed. We can only imagine how much greater you would have been if you hadn't been a cri— if you hadn't had problems with your spine."

"Some men have straight spines and twisted minds," Francis said.

"And some have tongues that are too big

for their mouths," said Neville. "Perhaps they should be cut down to size."

"Well, I think the Lancastrians would be happy to know we're sitting here in happy conversation instead of seeking them out for battle," I said. "Perhaps we can talk again when the enemy is defeated."

This time Neville did bow and, after shouting orders, the army rattled itself into readiness and then, with a lurch, rolled forward towards Hexham.

Obviously John Neville had decided our interview was over, and Francis, De Castile and I rode back to our own little unit of knights in silence. Neville was a surprising figure; he seemed to have all of the Earl of Warwick's energy and command, but none of his cleverness or ability to see where powerful friends could be made. He'd insulted me within minutes of meeting me and, though I was young, I was a prince and would one day grow up to have the sort of power that could be useful to him. Could such a man be trusted with command of an army?

Well, one thing was for sure, we would very soon find out!

CHAPTER NINE

We clattered along the road for the rest of the day. We were part of an army now that, though small, was obviously much larger than the unit of one hundred knights and squires that had left the Earl of Warwick's castle in Middleham, and as a result we moved much more slowly. There were many more wagons in the baggage train and even a few cannons and guns rattling along on their awkward wheels and pulled by horses. The guns were mainly small culverins, but there were one or two medium-sized serpentines too.

Slowly we rolled up the miles and at last the town of Hexham came into view. A great cry went up through the army because we knew the enemy were near. John Neville had been sending out scouts and they'd soon reported back that the Lancastrians were camped nearby, trying to block our route into Hexham itself.

Then at last, at a place with a fast-flowing river set between steep banks, with the appropriate name of Devil's Water, we saw them! They stood in three sections spread across flat meadowlands that probably would have been marshy in winter, but which were now were obviously dry and firm. One branch of the river protected their rear and another their front. I gazed at them hungrily. So this was the enemy! These were the people who would happily kill my brother the King and me as well if they could! They sparkled and glittered like a great fire as their armour and weapons flashed and glinted in

the sunlight. There seemed to be endless
thousands of them to me, but De Castile
dismissed them as a 'piddling little force'.

"They've chosen a good position though,"
he admitted.

We were sitting on high ground looking
down on them, and Francis leaned forward
eagerly in his saddle. "Yes, there are branches
of the river protecting them front and rear,

and they command good ground defending the only bridge over the water to Hexham."

"Exactly, my Lord Lovell," said De Castile. "The crossing's known locally as Linnels Bridge, and if John Neville's any sort of commander he'll know he's got to get the enemy out of there as soon as can be."

I looked to where Neville sat at a distance in conference with his officers. "We'll have to cross the river upstream somewhere and outflank them," I said quietly. "That way we'll gain access to the water meadow they're defending and all we'll need to do is push them back and take the bridge."

"Ah, I see we have a tactician with us," said De Castile kindly. "And you're right, we'll have to do exactly that. Cross the river in secret, and then take them by surprise in their flank or side. But now it's up to our commander to decide where and when."

Francis caught my eye and grinned in excitement. We'd hardly had time to discuss anything since setting out from Middleham. An army's not the most private of places to have a conversation. We didn't even share a tent so there'd been no chance to talk about anything at night. All we could do was snatch the occasional word when riding along.

Francis moved his horse closer now and, while De Castile rumbled on about strategies and troop movements, he leaned across. "Are you ready for all this?"

"For what?" I asked in turn. "You know we're only here to witness the action. We're not allowed to fight."

He shrugged with a clank of plate armour. "Strange things happen on a battlefield, we could get mixed up in the fighting without meaning to."

"And do you like that idea?" I asked.

Well, we're trained for it if that's what you mean," Francis replied.

"It's not, and it's not what you meant either."

"No," he agreed. "Sergeant Langham can tell you exactly how to kill a man, but actually doing it is a very different matter."

I nodded. We seemed to have been thinking about nothing else since we first learned we were going to battle. But no amount of discussion was ever going to prepare us for the reality.

"Well, one thing's for sure, Francis," I said with a smile. "If we do get 'mixed up in all the fighting' we're soon going to find out if we're ready for it... in fact probably in the next few hours."

That night we crossed the river. It was a moonless night and black as coal, but

Neville's men were well trained and followed their orders without question. We went a mile upstream and the noise of the rushing waters masked the sounds of horses, rumbling cannons and chinking armour.

The infantry crossed in boats that Neville had requisitioned from the local river folk and the cavalry took off their armour and that of the horses and then swam them across. The cannons were floated over on the flat-bottomed boats that were used as ferries and cargo carriers, and the cavalry's armour went with them.

One or two of the horses shied away from the cold water before being persuaded to plunge in, but everyone got across safely. Re-arming in the cold and dark with numb fingers was a struggle, but at last we were ready and whispered orders were passed along the line to set off for the Lancastrians' position. We made our way almost blind through the pitch dark, but a local guide knew the way and led us safely to the water meadow where the battle would be fought. With the first light of dawn we were drawn up and ready.

Once again the day was bright and clear, and the army that stood before us was brilliant with flags and the coats-of-arms of the cavalry.

My feelings were definitely mixed that morning, because De Castile and our force of one hundred knights and squires had left Francis and me sitting on a high hill looking down on the action, while they got ready to fight. Even Gisborough had been called to take part and had ridden off with them, his face an odd mingling of panic and pride.

Even though I'd known we weren't going to be allowed to fight I was still disappointed, but also I couldn't help being a little relieved. At least now I wouldn't have to kill anyone. Of course I'd never admit such a thing, not even to Francis, and for the next few minutes a struggle raged in my brain between the part of me that desperately wanted to fight, and the other part that was glad to be sitting out of it.

But then my attention was grabbed by movements down in the water meadow. I'd been told that the Duke of Somerset was in command of the enemy forces, and from my place on the piece of rising ground we'd occupied, I could see a gentleman riding up and down, shouting orders and pointing angrily at our position.

"My Lord of Somerset, I presume," I said.

"Yes, definitely," said one of the group of ten knights who'd been assigned as mine and Francis's personal bodyguards. "We must have been a terrible shock to wake up to!"

"He probably thinks he's having a nightmare, more like," said Francis.

"Well, we've certainly taken them by surprise," I said watching the officers scurrying about. "If Neville knows his job, he'll hit them now before they're ready."

Just as I said this, a trumpet sounded on the cool morning air and our cannons roared, sending shots smashing into the

Lancastrian ranks. The firing went on for a few minutes, throwing the enemy into chaos and confusion, then the combined force of our cavalry and infantry charged.

They hit the enemy's right wing like a glittering spear thrown by a giant, and a great clatter and clamour rose up into the air as men and horses screamed, sword hit sword, and lance smashed through shield into bone and soft flesh.

For a moment the enemy line held, but then suddenly they began to draw back, like a bank of fog before a strong wind. And then with a despairing roar they broke and soldiers were scrambling away, running for their lives back to the river and the bridge.

My face ached and I realized I was clenching my teeth with tension and excitement. Another trumpet sounded and we watched as Neville sent more of our army into the gap left by the fleeing enemy.

I could clearly see De Castile and the detachment of knights and squires from Middleham as they rolled forward down the hill and towards the enemy position. They moved slowly at first as they made sure everyone was together and then they gathered momentum as they moved down towards the river. Faster and faster they went until their horses leapt forward to fly in full gallop.

The enemy turned to face the Middleham cavalry, digging the butts of their spears into the ground and holding them at an angle. My ears were filled with the sounds of charging hooves, and of screaming men.

Our horses hit their line. A great roar went up and our cavalry drove forward, pushing the enemy back. The air was filled with arrows, crossbow bolts and flying spears. I saw our flag-bearer slump in his saddle and begin to fall. He held the standard he was carrying high, and his voice rang clear over the distance.

"FOR YORK! FOR YORK!"

Then as I watched, someone I recognized took the flag. Gisborough! The roar of onset sounded again as Neville led the rest of our army into the fight, and at last the enemy line began to waver until without warning they broke and ran.

Francis and I watched as our army pursued them to the bridge and to the steep banks of the river where many fell into the water in their desperation to get away from our chasing swords. Some tried to swim and drowned, dragged down by their armour, and others were crushed under the weight of their comrades as more and more fell down the banks.

A few tried to make a stand and turned to face our forces, but our army rode them down. Even though we were watching from such a distance the sunlight was brilliant and both of us could see that the bridge was packed with wounded and dying soldiers, but our own soldiers burst through and rode on, driving the defeated enemy before them.

Again in desperation some of the

Lancastrians turned to make a stand, but our horses drove through them. That was almost the last of the enemy's resistance and we watched as our soldiers pushed them along like sheep.

In fact we were so intent on watching the battle that no one in our small group noticed a fleeing band of nine or ten Lancastrian cavalry heading our way.

They galloped along a deep fold in the hill that rose towards our position and hid them from view. Suddenly they burst upon us, knocking two of our guardian knights from their saddles and hacking at us with battle-notched swords. There was hardly time to think; I snapped down my visor, drew my sword and thrust straight armed at the enemy knight before me. A lucky strike, the point found a gap in his armour and blood spurted out. He fell in a clatter of armour and, as I swung around, I saw Francis smash his mace down onto the head of another Lancastrian. He dropped like a stone.

Now together with our remaining bodyguards we drove forward, killing as we went. It was over in seconds. Six of their knights lay dead and two of ours. Four of them escaped.

I lifted my visor and grinned at Francis. Despite all the efforts to keep us out of the fighting we'd been blooded after all.

CHAPTER TEN

By nightfall we were in an armed camp in the hills. In the distance we could hear our soldiers celebrating the Yorkist victory in the streets of Hexham, a sight that wasn't considered fit for boys of our age. The actual fighting had been brief, and De Castile said it was little more than a big skirmish, but it would stay with Francis and me throughout our lives.

Our forces had taken possession of Hexham Castle and Neville had made the Great Hall his main centre of operations. Later that night a messenger came from the town and told us many of the Lancastrian leaders were brought to what Neville called justice.

It wasn't really a trial. Neville just asked for their names and then sent them off to be executed. No one objected, not even the prisoners themselves. The messenger said they even looked like men who were already dead, with blank eyes and pale faces. In the end over thirty were killed.

Later, after the messengers had gone back to Hexham, Francis and I sat over a campfire and discussed what we'd heard.

"Well, at least that's thirty fewer Lancastrian leaders to trouble us in the future," my friend said as he lowered himself painfully to the ground. After a day and a night in the saddle both of us had aching muscles.

"Or thirty fewer new allies made loyal by a pardon," I finally answered, after I too had carefully sat down and found a comfortable position for my back. "My brother has forgiven his enemies before now, and some have served faithfully ever since."

Francis shrugged. "It's a difficult one; how can you tell who will remain loyal in gratitude and who will secretly think you weak for not carrying out the obvious punishment? What would you have done?"

I didn't answer for a long time as I considered the question, but then I said: "What can I say? They were the enemy of the House of York, and therefore the enemy of my brother. Perhaps I'd have done the same if

I'd been in Neville's place, and perhaps the Lancastrians would have done the same to us if they'd won. But I can't help wondering if we've killed men who one day could have been useful friends and allies."

"Well, it's too late now," Francis replied bluntly. "They're just food for worms."

I shuddered. How many others would die before this war finally ended?

The next day dawned grey and drizzly. The streets of Hexham were quiet at last. With his usual discipline, De Castile had ordered an early start for our journey back to Middleham, and though a few of the men had sore heads, everyone who'd survived the battle and could ride was in the saddle at first light.

Our own casualties had been light, only five knights had been killed and eight squires, though a few more than that were wounded, including Gisborough, who had a deep sword cut in his arm. He and the other injured were placed in a wagon with two monks from the Hexham priory infirmary to look after them on the journey. Gisborough's wounds weren't as bad as we first thought, and already he was sitting up and demanding to be allowed to ride, so I was more than hopeful he'd soon make a full recovery.

John Neville didn't bother to see us off, a further example of his bad manners, but I suppose I couldn't expect too much from a man who was the brother of the Earl of Warwick. In fact we clattered away with hardly anyone to see us go. Nobody waved and nobody cheered, and when we rode by the battlefield the dead remained silent.

Our own dead already lay in a mass grave dug immediately after the fighting. In fact it was still being filled in as we went by, so we did get a few waves from the gravediggers as we made our way home.

I soon found that the time after combat is quiet and sad, or quiet and full of horror. The joy of battle I'd heard veteran soldiers talk of soon fades and leaves behind it an empty space that everyone fills in their own way.

We camped that night in exactly the same place as we had when riding to Hexham, but this time there was no real need to set guards and pickets, though De Castile insisted on them.

Neither Francis nor I had much to say to each other, we just felt deadly tired and that night he shared my tent, both of us glad to know there was someone else nearby.

CHAPTER ELEVEN

The next day dawned sunny, and with it came a lightening of our moods. We'd soon be home, we'd won our first battle and we knew there'd be a victory feast waiting to greet us because De Castile had sent riders ahead while the rest of the detachment kept pace with the wagon of the wounded.

I couldn't wait to see Anne again and tell her at least some of the details of the fighting. I didn't want to say too much about the blood and the horrible chaos of it all, not because I didn't think she was strong enough to hear such things, but because I didn't want to remember it myself.

We made steady progress throughout the day and, though we didn't move as fast as we had on the way to Hexham, we slowly ate up the miles until the landscape became more and more familiar and soon we knew we were within striking distance of Middleham Castle.

De Castile had insisted that we all wore full armour, even though we were in no danger now, because this way we'd look splendid as we rode into the castle.

Francis had eagerly entered the spirit of things and made a point of putting an extra polish on his breastplate and helmet, and he even wore the decorative chain that showed he was a baron that he must have hidden in the baggage train somewhere.

"I've seen acrobats at a fair that glittered less than you," I said.

"Thank you," he answered and grinned.

"It wasn't meant as a compliment," I said. "All you need is an apple in your mouth and you'd look like a roast piglet at a banquet!"

He frowned and I waited for the insult to be returned. But instead he stared along the road that ran as straight as an arrow across the moorland. "What's that?" He asked nodding ahead.

I looked along the road, shading my eyes. "I don't know... horses, I think... probably just a farmer on his way to market."

"No, I see the glint of weapons!" He turned and waved up De Castile who was further back down the line shouting at a squire who wasn't dressed to the standard he wanted.

The old soldier rode forward and joined us. "I do believe the Earl of Warwick has sent an escort to greet us," he said after staring ahead.

"No. It's not that," I answered. "There are only two soldiers and what looks like…" I paused as I narrowed my eyes. "And what looks like two women!"

De Castile immediately ordered that we all rode as smartly as we could, or, as he put it, "in full martial readiness."

Soon the riders were near enough to be made out clearly and then one of the women suddenly let out a squeal of delight and galloped ahead of the others. It was then that I recognized her.

"It's Anne," I said grinning at Francis. "It's Anne come to meet us!"

Her neat little pony thundered down on us and she expertly pulled it up to a standstill before it could crash into our heavily armoured horses. "You're back! You're here! What was it like? Did you fight? Were you valiant and noble?"

I laughed at the tumble of questions. "Valiant and noble? Francis!? No he fought like a drunk defending his beer in a brawl!"

"And you fought like a dancer; all neat and clean before making a kill that looked like a mother telling off her child for being naughty!" he answered with a laugh.

I shrugged. "But it was a kill nonetheless."

"Are you hurt?" Anne went on. "Were your lives ever in danger?"

But before we could answer, an old lady on a fat pony came wheezing up. "Mistress Anne Neville, what would the Earl and your mother say if they could see the way you are behaving at this moment?"

This was Anne's chaperone, whose job it was to ensure she behaved like a lady.

"They probably would be too busy asking the same questions as me to notice how I was behaving," she answered coolly.

"Be that as may be," the fat old lady answered. "I only agreed to this ride to meet our army if it was conducted with proper behaviour and seemly manners."

"Have I been unseemly then?" Anne asked, her eyes wide with innocence.

"I would say that galloping your pony to meet the soldiers was less than ladylike, yes!"

"Well, I think I was simply showing a fitting pleasure in their safe return as befits even the most well-behaved lady," Anne answered sharply. "And anyway, stop interrupting the Prince, he was about to say something!"

The old lady went into a flutter and I grinned at Anne. "In answer to your question, Mistress Neville, all of our lives were in danger, and no, neither Francis nor I were hurt, though Gisborough is amongst the wounded."

That caused a great explosion of flapping hands and ponies clip clopping down to the wounded to ensure Gisborough was truly mending. But once the ladies had ensured that was the case, we all moved on towards the castle and home.

"There's to be a victory banquet tonight, of course," said Anne and smiled brilliantly. "There's to be musicians and acrobats and dancing…"

"And food I hope!" said Francis.

"Lots of food. The cooks have been baking and roasting and frying since dawn this morning! I think even Baron Francis Lovell will find himself as stuffed as a goose!"

"Good. I need my food after everything that's happened."

"Then perhaps we can all meet again later," Anne went on, looking over her shoulder to where her chaperone was giggling like a girl with De Castile. "Perhaps in your chambers before the banquet, Richard, where you can tell me all the details without interruptions from someone who thinks it's not ladylike for me to hear about such things."

At that point the first flags of Middleham Castle rose over the horizon and I could just make out the design of the bear and the ragged staff that was the Earl of Warwick's insignia.

"We'll tell you everything we can remember, Anne," I said. Then added to myself quietly. "Or at least as much as we can bring ourselves to say."

EPILOGUE

The lives of Richard, Anne and Francis were not to end happily, though for a time all seemed to go well. Richard and Anne married in 1472 and had a son named Edward. Richard became a great military leader, fighting in several battles against the Lancastrians. He also led a war against Scotland, during which he captured the town of Berwick-Upon-Tweed in 1482.

In April 1483, Richard's brother King Edward IV died and Richard was crowned King on 6th of July of the same year. But then in April 1484, his son Edward died and in the following year so too did his wife, Anne.

Richard continued to rule, but the Lancastrian Henry Tudor raised an army against him, and on the 22nd of August

1485 the Battle of Bosworth was fought. Here Richard died fighting for his crown, the last English King to be killed in battle. Even his enemies say that he died bravely leading a charge against Henry Tudor.

Francis Lovell remained a loyal friend to Richard throughout his life. He became Lord Chamberlain and a Knight of the Garter in 1483. After the Battle of Bosworth, Francis escaped and led a revolt in Yorkshire against the new King, Henry Tudor. When this failed he fled to Flanders, but returned in 1487 to fight against Henry once more at the Battle of Stoke Field. The Yorkists were defeated again and some say Lovell escaped to Scotland. No one knows when or how Francis died, though one tradition says he was buried in All Hallows Church in Nottinghamshire, having died of his wounds after the Battle of Stoke Field.

HOUSE OF YORK
FAMILY TREE

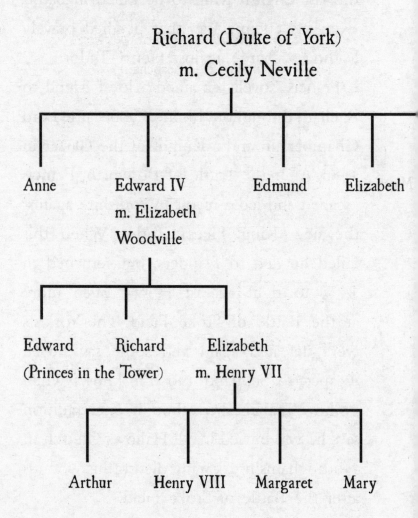

Richard (Duke of York)
m. Cecily Neville

Anne   Edward IV   Edmund   Elizabeth

m. Elizabeth

Woodville

Edward   Richard   Elizabeth

(Princes in the Tower)   m. Henry VII

Arthur   Henry VIII   Margaret   Mary

Richard Warwick (Earl of Warwick)

m. Anne de Beauchamp

Margaret   George   Richard III

m. Isobel   m. Anne

Neville   Neville

Edward   Margaret   Edward

(Earl of Warwick)   (Prince of Wales)